HOPSCOTCH

Clever Cat

First published in 2003 by
Franklin Watts
338 Euston Road
London
NW1 3BH

Franklin Watts Australia
Level 17 / 207 Kent Street
Sydney
NSW 2000

A CIP catalogue record for this book is available
from the British Library.

ISBN 978 0 7496 5131 2

Series Editor: Jackie Hamley
Series Advisor: Dr Barrie Wade
Cover Design: Jason Anscomb
Design: Peter Scoulding

Printed in China

Franklin Watts is a division of
Hachette Children's Books,
an Hachette Livre UK company.

For Dave the cat – KW

Clever Cat

by Karen Wallace and Anni Axworthy

FRANKLIN WATTS
LONDON • SYDNEY

Clever Cat dances with his head in the air. "I've got a tail like a wolf," he cries. "My eyes are green as a dragon!"

Old Mother Goose

waggles her wings.

Nanny Goat rolls
her strange eyes.

"You're a silly young cat,"
quacks Mr Duck. "You should
be out catching mice.

You should be out hunting rats.
Not dancing about with your head
in the air!"

Clever Cat grins. He doesn't care.
"You're a bunch of old fusspots,"
he cries. And he tickles their noses
as he swishes his tail.

"I'm telling the farmer!" squawks
Old Mother Goose.

Nanny Goat nods and blows through her nose. "What good is a cat with a tail like a wolf?"

Mr Duck shakes his fine feathered head. "Who cares if his eyes are as green as a dragon?"

That night, a huge moon rises over the farmyard. Tucked up in bed, the farmer snores and turns over.

He doesn't see the hungry fox trot
over the meadow. He doesn't hear
the gate creak and swing open.

Clever Cat is awake.

He hides in the shadows.

He sees the hungry fox
creep over the farmyard.

Old Mother Goose shivers and shakes. The goat and the duck huddle beside her.

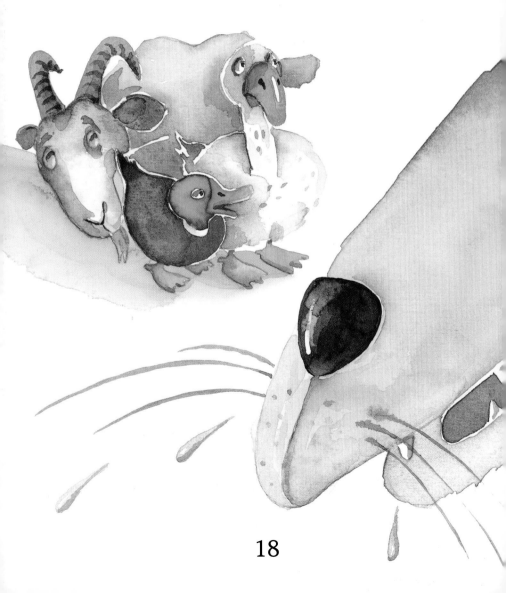

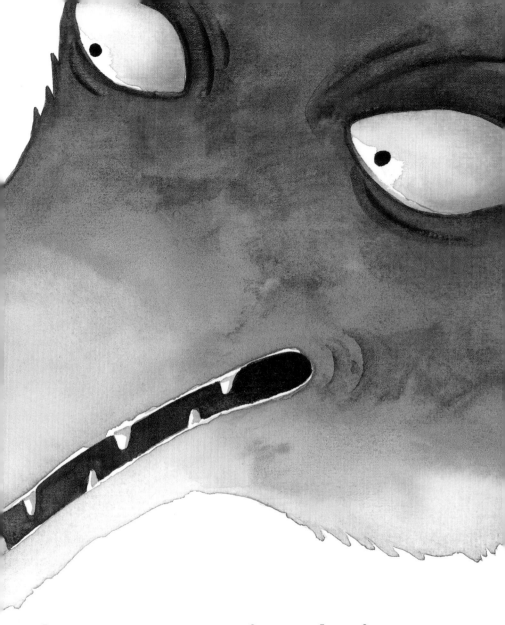

They want to run from the fox,
but they are frozen like statues.

The hungry fox drools. He creeps closer and closer. Will he eat...

...a goose,

or a goat,

or a duck

for his supper?

Clever Cat jumps! In the glow of the
moon, his tail is huge like a wolf.

By the light of the stars, his eyes are green like a dragon.

"Help!" cries the fox. "It's a wolf! It's a dragon!

His heart bangs in his chest.

His legs tremble like jelly.

The frightened
fox turns and
runs from the
farmyard.

Old Mother Goose waggles her
wings. Nanny Goat blinks her
strange eyes.

"You're a wonder, you are," quacks
Mr Duck. "We're sorry we called
you a silly young cat."

29

Clever Cat grins. He doesn't care.
He dances about with his head
in the air!

30

Hopscotch has been specially designed to fit the requirements of the National Literacy Strategy. It offers real books by top authors and illustrators for children developing their reading skills. There are 49 Hopscotch stories to choose from:

Marvin, the Blue Pig
ISBN 978 0 7496 4619 6

Plip and Plop
ISBN 978 0 7496 4620 2

The Queen's Dragon
ISBN 978 0 7496 4618 9

Flora McQuack
ISBN 978 0 7496 4621 9

Willie the Whale
ISBN 978 0 7496 4623 3

Naughty Nancy
ISBN 978 0 7496 4622 6

Run!
ISBN 978 0 7496 4705 6

The Playground Snake
ISBN 978 0 7496 4706 3

"Sausages!"
ISBN 978 0 7496 4707 0

Bear in Town
ISBN 978 0 7496 5875 5

Pippin's Big Jump
ISBN 978 0 7496 4710 0

Whose Birthday Is It?
ISBN 978 0 7496 4709 4

The Princess and the Frog
ISBN 978 0 7496 5129 9

Flynn Flies High
ISBN 978 0 7496 5130 5

Clever Cat
ISBN 978 0 7496 5131 2

Moo!
ISBN 978 0 7496 5332 3

Izzie's Idea
ISBN 978 0 7496 5334 7

Roly-poly Rice Ball
ISBN 978 0 7496 5333 0

I Can't Stand It!
ISBN 978 0 7496 5765 9

Cockerel's Big Egg
ISBN 978 0 7496 5767 3

How to Teach a Dragon Manners
ISBN 978 0 7496 5873 1

The Truth about those Billy Goats
ISBN 978 0 7496 5766 6

Marlowe's Mum and the Tree House
ISBN 978 0 7496 5874 8

The Truth about Hansel and Gretel
ISBN 978 0 7496 4708 7

The Best Den Ever
ISBN 978 0 7496 5876 2

ADVENTURE STORIES

Aladdin and the Lamp
ISBN 978 0 7496 6692 7

Blackbeard the Pirate
ISBN 978 0 7496 6690 3

George and the Dragon
ISBN 978 0 7496 6691 0

Jack the Giant-Killer
ISBN 978 0 7496 6693 4

TALES OF KING ARTHUR

1. The Sword in the Stone
ISBN 978 0 7496 6694 1

2. Arthur the King
ISBN 978 0 7496 6695 8

3. The Round Table
ISBN 978 0 7496 6697 2

4. Sir Lancelot and the Ice Castle
ISBN 978 0 7496 6698 9

TALES OF ROBIN HOOD

Robin and the Knight
ISBN 978 0 7496 6699 6

Robin and the Monk
ISBN 978 0 7496 6700 9

Robin and the Silver Arrow
ISBN 978 0 7496 6703 0

Robin and the Friar
ISBN 978 0 7496 6702 3

FAIRY TALES

The Emperor's New Clothes
ISBN 978 0 7496 7421 2

Cinderella
ISBN 978 0 7496 7417 5

Snow White
ISBN 978 0 7496 7418 2

Jack and the Beanstalk
ISBN 978 0 7496 7422 9

The Three Billy Goats Gruff
ISBN 978 0 7496 7420 5

The Pied Piper of Hamelin
ISBN 978 0 7496 7419 9

HISTORIES

Toby and the Great Fire of London
ISBN 978 0 7496 7079 5 *
ISBN 978 0 7496 7410 6

Pocahontas the Peacemaker
ISBN 978 0 7496 7080 1 *
ISBN 978 0 7496 7411 3

Grandma's Seaside Bloomers
ISBN 978 0 7496 7081 8 *
ISBN 978 0 7496 7412 0

Hoorah for Mary Seacole
ISBN 978 0 7496 7082 5 *
ISBN 978 0 7496 7413 7

Remember the 5th of November
ISBN 978 0 7496 7083 2 *
ISBN 978 0 7496 7414 4

Tutankhamun and the Golden Chariot
ISBN 978 0 7496 7084 9 *
ISBN 978 0 7496 7415 1

* **hardback**